# THE FENCE BETWEEN DREAM AND LIFE

## THE FABLE

SUMEET KUMAR

ISBN 979-888530864-9

## *Sumeet Kumar*

**Sumeet Kumar,** A adult who experiences many phases of love in his life , get broked many times , stands up everytime and keep moving to the next phases of the life. In reality he is a writter as well as singer (as a hobby). Very exciting and interesting fact about him is that he is a author of New era i.e. he starts his journey of writing at the age when he was going to schools to get the study.

His some famous works i.e. Maturity Of Love (Genre - Love), Privacy For Dream (Genre - Middle Class), Army Squad of Love (Genre- The Seperation of Army Love), 5 Days of Love (Genre- Temporarily Love), Th e Endearment Of Love (Genre - Historical Era Of Love), Social Destruction Indo-Pak (Genre - The Story of The Love At The Time Of Division Of India And Pakistan), Middle Class Soul (Genre - The Dreams of Middle Class), The Accursed Kanatpur (Genre - The Horrific Story Of A Village), Wrong Number (Genre - The Suspenseful Physco Killer Story), The Secrecy Of Deadly Midnight (Genre - The Suspense About a Crime), Fragile Religious Of Death (Genre- The Death Of A Trustful Person), Nature Vs Science (Genre - The Future Battle Between Nature And Science In A Horrific Way), Generic Man (Genre - The Dream of I.I.T), The Unconsious 12 Hours (Genre - The Illusion At Stage Of Comma), The Strange Burden (Genre - The Burden Of Love) , Her Existence (Genre - The Femlae Pain In The Society) , Jockstrap Prize (Genre - The True Story Of A National Athlete). are available on various geners on the offcial platform of Amazon, Flipkart and Notionpress. You can buy them from there.

# Contents

# Preface

***The Fence Between Dream And Life.***

if you have forgotten something you can learn it again but if you lose something you can't be able to .... it Too must have come, not what it means, we know what our dreams are, I do a lot to fulfill those dreams, but the condition becomes such that we have to excuse us every time. We get that I want to fly ...., but I do not have the hope that I can see and move forward. Every day we bash think that today or tomorrow will change, but that time does not take the name of changing, because instead of improving with time, the condition gets worse and worse, so this is not a story of any one person, but listen to it all. After all, it will happen that we all talk about this and this condition matches. So this story is about a boy who tries every day, he will try to get out of his condition, but every time there is some trouble in front of him. It used to come in front of him that he used to accept the same defeat but there was a specialty in that he used to give up at that time but next time he would try to forget everything and try to fly once again for the flight of his dream. He knew that his dreams would not be fulfilled, yet trying became a habit with time. He used to break every day but try to connect himself again the next day. Why do we wait so much for this, let's stay dry and understand this autobiography.

# ACKNOWLEDGEMENTS

***Aman Kumar***

Special Thanks to **Aman Kumar** who worked so hard in the preparation of this book. He has continually put with my passi ve voice, omission of words, and late night calls. You have be en wonderful. Thanks to him for his precious time in reviewing proposals , individual chap ters and early drafts, along with his suggestions on the applicability of the material to the world.

# I

# The Road To Make Virtual to Reality

Born on 15 March 2003 to a middle class family a little boy named Dhruv .... A name that was only on a dreamer boy .... But what did he know when my name meant that would change further .... his parents None of the family members lived together, he was also a middle class family .... Dhruv's dad lived in a typical middle class family where there was no room for dreams, only his family believed that he could somehow make ends meet. Complete and take a job .... His father had four brothers and Dhruv's father was the youngest of them all and his father, I mean Dhruv's grandfather, was a head in the panchayat, which we know in the village (the head name is chief). Dhruv's father always lived in the village (accessory) with his sisters and was always engaged in household chores (Dhruv was born about a year after Dhruv's Grand Father (Grandfather died ....) .... Dhruv's mother also used to live in a typical middleclass family where girls wanted to dream only to do one thing, they were taught from childhood how to do housework and how to make your in-laws happy (which is today It is a trend of yesterday and old times) .... Dhruv's mother was the eldest in the house and one of his family was his brother and the other was his daughter and other family members lived in the village and Dhruv's maternal grandfather was a farmer (farmer) ) and his mother was a housewife .... and one of the strangest thing was that only his brother was sent to school in his house and everyone else lived in the house which means that the flight of dreams was that of Dhruv at the time of his parents. I had been weak since then, or just say that the fate of such a thread, whose breaking was already decided .... My only wish is to say that the time has changed. If we change our condition then .... Well let's go ahead and see who else, what new peacocks are seen in Dhruv's story .... Dhruv's family was a big family in which he got all 10 people and he was the youngest in the house just like his dad's family .... before this Dhruv's family faced a lot of difficulties so let's take a look at that too and let's complete the story where the story was incomplete a little earlier.... .

# II

# The Short Of Consciousness

1996... Seven years before Dhruv's birth, his family was in such a condition that no human being can describe in words. It is said that in middle class family, there is more hope than dreams, often what we want. They come to our part, they keep coming and coming .... Every middle class family has the same profession .... In today's time, just by studying, you engineer this doctor, this bank clerk, pass this general competition and take a government job .... us We do not get enough flight that we can spread the wings of our dreams .... Relationships in middle class family are like glass, if you press lightly on it, it will break, 23 April 1999 From that day till today, a lot of ups and downs Offers have come to Dhruv's family, as when Dhruv's great uncle told this to his brothers, what will you do by staying here? After all, his grandfather was a headman and he had a lot of land and as long as he was there, no one had any problem, but After his departure, Dhruv's father faced a lot of problems, .... as when he was separated from his family, he had been married for 29 years and Dhruv's brother Behen had grown up quite a lot, in the begining When Dhruv's father left his accessory and came to city, he was ...., so he had to spend the night on road for many days, because at that time he did not have a job, nor did he have enough money to live in a rented house for himself. .... At that time all his children and Dhruv's mother were not with him because they were all in the secondary .... His father stopped him by saying that when I get work, I will come to pick up everyone myself .... Many days and many nights Dhruv's father sees the same disappointment every day when he doesn't get work as a sun sinks without its light .... There comes a time in everyone's life where we give up our hope, the destination is close to it .... But Dhruv's father did not do this, nor could he give up his hope, nor could he forget the words of his brothers and finally did whatever they wanted. They were looking for what they finally got .... Just like this .... If the branch and route of a tree will be week then the whole tree will be week .... When Dhruv's father has to face so many difficulties and the same to his family Even facing many difficulties, mercury is .... May not say that people of every middle class family are bad but the family of Dhruv used to mean more money than relationships, yes it is also that in today's time people spend money. Gives more value than relationship .... Even in his family, his uncle and his wife have caused many sorrows to their mother, sometimes they did not even give her food. Dhruv's brothers and sisters left many nights without eating and drinking .... but they say that time changes everyone but no one expects it because the day the hope will come to know, the day will not change at all .... They had this good news. Sometime we will overcome this darkness and the condition we are in now will also change .... We have seen so many heroes in movies but in real life we get to see a lot of work .... A lot of time has passed but the condition was the same. Dhruv's father was a 12$^{th}$ fail candidate after all, so he got a job that too a government job, it was very difficult at that time I already told you that he never stolen his hope .... After about 7 months, he got a driver He got a job and finally fulfilled what he promised his children They have come, there is still a long time to complete them.....

***“"if you get the time***
***The condition will definitely change (2)***
***And the dream that had been missed***
***somewhere in the middle***

***Will change his flight again......."***"

# III

# The Total Money Breakdown

In the middle class family, dreams are more likely to be pure at work nowadays, because dreams are a way to be visible to the world and to make an identity of yourself, nowadays in the .... world, you have to learn how to live from someone. Can learn from middle class family .... because it is such a mixture where sometimes there is happiness and sometimes there is sorrow .... Time change but their hopes never change, They can change their paths but they can never change their dreams, for a short time .... middle class family lives every day with the same hope that today's chance is gone but tomorrow it will come again. There is a very good proverb in my language which you want to hear.

"

***"What did you expect from you?***
***dreams have many awakenings***
***leave your own way, brother***
***Other's path is banbait ........."*** "

I also belong from a middle class family and every middle class family who thinks that when they grow up their son will make their name bright, it is still said in my family .... many work people get this opportunity to do their work. Don't let the dream make you a dream .... But I had said one thing earlier that every little song of middle class family is made of adulteration in which sometimes happiness and sometimes sorrow comes .... Our biggest mistake is this that we believe more than ourselves in those who may not even those whom people consider to be treacherous these days .... May not saying that I am an atheist or I do not trust them .... May I want to say that whatever we wish to puree your dreams To take it upon ourselves, there is also a hidden belief in that which gives us the vision of God .... then why should we hand over our hope to some stone and give our hard work to someone else's name .... I do not accept it It is because no parent, instead of raising them from your child, keeps a wish from them that they should also take care of them. .... They made us not we them .... Our hope is that they are not weakness, well let's move things forward and what his father has done in Dhruv's family, how does he take his family with him...... ..

# IV
# Middle Class Hero

Not a single day happened in those three years that I can tell you that something has changed in his life in those three years, well he says no (every moment is connected with a new situation) no one but me can say these things

Because after that, no one can guess the condition that changed for them .... Yes, after all, their condition changed a little but for some time, but for some time it had become a whole life for them, or au say that complete happiness Only for some time but they had it, which was neither under pressure nor due to anyone's compulsion, nor was it found .... after losing anything, so the only reason was that their struggle (if the way If it is bad, it does not mean that we forget our destination) Or say that when the relationship is broken with something, then try to connect them, not to break them .... yes relationship was in those three years where no ordinary house Despite this, he spent his days at the house of struggle, no one even supported him, but his hard work was great, when there was nothing to eat but the time was for himself. Treating restlessness as hunger and trying to eliminate it, how can we say that there was no relationship ....

"

***"you didn't have a relationship***
***yet he supported***
***when there was nothing to lose***
***I still held on ,***
***Still didn't feel the absence***
***The innings that was happiness in those hands***
***Donated everything as soon as she asked for it(2)***
...."

I have probably forgotten to tell something to all of you that there was a time in their life when someone said that quote You give your child to us .That's just because his brother who was older than Dhruv was very handsome and who said this time he had only one child and she was also a girl .... So sometimes I don't understand what happiness gives to others Making the condition of a marginal character ...., I was infatuated with them for a long time, but why .... why girls are not handsome, they cannot act like boys .... It is necessary that only a boy should carry forward one's lineage) There was also a problem at that time that they (Dhruv's family) did not even have enough money to take care of everyone well, so they were also forced to say nothing .... at the time they also did not say anything to them .... at the time. There is no one like a mother, after all, what Dhruv's mother said is the highest in today's era .... Dhruv's mother said that you also have a daughter, can you give it to anyone, bash is enough was to shut his tongue .... then what was it that disappeared from him as if I am a believer of some kind .... Why would anyone give his child to anyone, after all, he kept it under the shade of his mother for 9 months.

"

***"Break the threads of love***
***when mother's love spreads ...."***"

.... means it is quite simple that no one's attachment to a mother's love lasts, even if it is her own) ....

Some words are made for mother.....

"

***"the reason for your love***
***Since we have walked in the ways***
***If you will not be there then who are we?***

,

***no pain is hidden from you***
***Cause whenever I make eye contact***
***Every time i finds silence***
***that i can't even see,***
***I know mom your lap has made me so strong***
***that if there is any obstacle , i'll pass through it***
***But the sound of your leaving,***
***then my own arms will fire up this world."***"

# V

# The Happy Pulses

On the day of June 14, 2003, a new peacock came in Dhruv's family, whenever I remember this day, I get a lot of agriculture that even though it took time to get out of those situations, finally Dhruv's family crossed those conditions and created a new one. Was waiting in the mornining about to be born, then a lot of trouble came, because at that time there was neither a doctor nor any such person who could get the delivery done and it was raining heavily from above that someone Ambulance was also difficult to come .... time but it was evening time .... There was little work with a hero .... On this day, the wind was blowing so closely that the light that the candle tried to bring, it did not last long, all were in the dark and nothing was clearly visible, equally late In me Dhruv's mother got up to drink water that his foot slipped (but it is good that he fell new, at that time Dhruv's father completely took his hand. had taken love, how romantic that moment would be .... at all, I was also thinking that something like this would have happened but nothing like this happened) When her foot slipped, then she started labor pains (meaning labor pain started ....) Then did all the people who were in their homes after hearing their voice and ran away without seeing how much it is raining, this wind is blowing loudly (To be honest, Indian women are very full without thinking anything) I salute them for their bravery) Well let's look ahead, so when everyone came to hear their voices, there were also some shameless people who did not mean anything to them ... after a while the pain was so much It has increased that now there is no other option but to give home. And what were the emotions, no one can tell, all the people were very happy, the same person also asked whether there was a boy or a girl (if he had lived at the right time, then the person first Explains too much .... What is the meaning of asking such a question that a boy has happened that what a girl should do on ...., the habit of some people cannot be changed because such people are beyond our understanding (society), the answer will also come in a while. father said that at that time a son has happened in my house .... Everyone may know that the elder son or daughter of the house, people call their parents by their name .... Dhruv's father was so happy that as if some treasure was in hand what to do on their .... But the profit coming from it makes a difference) .... Yes, his neighbor Nath ji was like that .... He didn't mean anything except sweets, Dhruv's father had not even seen Dhruv's face and he had appealed to eat .... After a few days he came to see the face of our hero (Big eyes, a different smile on his face, and his eyes were so sweet that there was no match in this world at the time, his hands were so soft that in front of which there was nothing even cotton and what was needed .... all Were very happy, Dhruv's father Dhruv's brother sisters and his small world .... and someone knew that Dhruv has also brought his all happiness with you (if he knew when he spoke, imagine what he would say .... I think) So it says that papa has become a lot of struggle now bash has become a lot of struggle now .... .... what a happy day it was for him, only those who have gone through the condition will understand this apart from him .... well was a little emotional Let's go ahead and see what happiness Dhruv's arrival brings in his world.

# VI

# The Gradual Conversion Of Memory to Happiness

A few days after the birth of Dhruv, he got a government job and also 50 thousand rupees and the dreams that Dhruv's father had seen, probably all of them were going to be fulfilled now .... such as (one uncle house, one good job) And a good future for his entire family and his children .... I had said earlier that as much as our dreams do not grow up in the middle class, their hopes are bigger .... There was something similar in Dhruv's family as well because Dhruv's father said this So thought that how to do it but when to do it did not know what they would do because the life they had lived before it was very bad but the life which has changed with the arrival of Dhruv

maybe it was quite different if from the earlier one
Compare ....

"

***"Things have changed***
***Not luck (2).***
***And what I ask from God everyday in worship***
***He does not even have the handwriting of his fate."***"

In the first 4 years, there was no problem because his father now had a government job and money was also getting very good and now he also had a good house and he is not a speaker to them but home too So, now Dhruv's father had achieved the place on rent, perhaps he saved him from the rest of the trouble: .... but I had said earlier also that the condition has changed, luck is not .... Well I will tell you directly what to say by turning around, Dhruv was now 4 years old and like the rest of the children, he was quite different because most of the children insist to play or go out somewhere but our Dhruv was probably the first child who had more value to know school because when all his brothers When sisters used to go to school, a thought had arisen in him too that all the schools go to college and he stays at home .... what was then, after talking about me, he told everyone one day that too. Why don't you read all of you in front of dad, why not me .... on this question, first of all people are very upset and his father also gives few words on .... In the end, all of them lost their lives in a single thought .... What was then, after thinking for a long time, after a few days, finally our Dhruv also got admission in a school where his brother sister was already studying .... me even today Remember, he was very happy that day and in the whole locality he had made a noise that he too would go to school from tomorrow, he would also get new bags, new bottles and new books .... dreams were not big but his blowing was big enough not to do anything big I wanted to be equal to everyone, but today it feels bad to think that she is no longer with us, that margin is not with us, her angry eyes are not with us, I may have prepared it too. I am not that the boy who tried to move forward every day by drooling from all the situations, he would really lose one day .... The texture of childhood is just like water, if we mix anything in it then it takes its place .... Well Now is not the right time for all of you to know that when all this happened and why he is not with us, because he may make his story incomplete. Can't leave because your feelings have been added to it, so let's go ahead and see what happens in our Dhruv's life ....

"

***"come i wish you were with me***
***it was a spring of happiness***
***life may look new***
***Still you would have a hand in that identity***
***All we are saying is without you***
***Those are some memories of yours which are in***
***this dead body***
***I have died so far***
***but how can we tell you***
***if these memories don't last***
***So the place of this dead body would have been***
***equal."***"

# VII

# Money Makes You Clever

Childhood's texture has no shape, it will mold as you mold it, well let it remain the same because all this is a matter of knowledge and to a large extent it is true and to a large extent it is also a lie. It is .... but Dhruv's story was a story that had a place in childhood but probably was not ahead of it .... I remember that day but don't remember the way (date) when Dhruv went to school for the first time, I mean his The first day was .... in school, many times it happens that if children get what they want, then later they do not appreciate it at all, but our pole was not like that because whatever he wished for, he would fulfill it. was .... Dhruv was a bright student since childhood he knew that life does not give us any second chance because everyone gets it only once and in this we have to move forward and also with it (time and life are very similar) Because we get both of them only once). He knew how his whole family had gone through the circumstances, so he did not want to look back at Moore, even though he was 4 years old, but his thoughts were not at all like a 4 year old child, it was quite different, the time no one knew better how to walk with .... and one thing he always said Because he used to say that good memories only give happiness, no one sees the reason behind it, but if memories are poets and are painful, then people appreciate them, they want to improve them .... Had a very different childhood. Even after topping for years, his desire remained the reason for him to move forward .... He says that no one who aspires for his destination has a lot of difficulties in his way Even if .... then it could not have happened that .... is a scientific thing which probably Whether I understand it or not, still I want to tell, they say here that his face matches his because it is his own blood, but why no one says that his troubles meet him, his efforts meet them .... Everyone will tell, but no one tells how to walk on them because the biggest mistake of today is that we have forgotten humanity, if a person is successful then we can follow his life .... If he is not successful then he should be our work Not .... Dhruv's life was so hard that it was very difficult for him to walk on it and also for others seeing him because along with childhood memories, there are some such memories which hurt a lot and Dhruv's memories The thing that bothered him the most was that his destination would never change and even if it did change, he could not change it by looking at those circumstances, but perhaps these things or luck was acceptable to him, but not his destiny at all (he Everyone says that luck and fortune are in the hands of the one above. .... I have said that Dhruv did not say these things, but whatever is in your hands. If you are close to him and have the desire to lose him, then it is only possible to believe in the lights at the time, even if you don't want to. Its illusion is not stealing us .... In today's era we can buy everything (Emotion Feeling Career Relationship I mean whatever thing we got this nature has given, we can buy everything by stealing only one thing that is someone) Death and someone's life is .... and the only reason for all of me is money (money is .... and nothing else) .... but there is nothing wrong with it, if seen from my point of view, then I would like to say that people talk about supporting They do but when the time comes, because of some paper (money) they also get away in the middle. .... And for Dhruv too, the only trouble was money (Which is the wish of every middle class family nowadays .... Dhruv) never thought that because of some piece of paper, all his dreams, his destination, his dreams, his efforts would be lost .....

***"If it was difficult, it would still go on but it would be a mistake.***

***the destination before her stole my feet of success from me."*"**

# VIII

# The Essence of Change

We are not compelled when everything is snatched from us, we are compelled when our own words and Anshul (Adarsh) and our own soul (Soul) also shatters us .... Dhruva is not revenge but his family Whatever past he had and whatever poetic memories he had or whatever he faced in the past, everything is now happening with Dhruv (life is not a part of the revelation but the moments and sacrifice is a part of the revelation when They are like gotta stability) .... I had said that there is a scientific word which we know as genetics, because genetics is the only thing that Dhruv's family had suffered by his brother sisters. All that was going to happen with Dhruv now, so why wait, let's see at what point Dhruv's life has come. After many days of good health, now the lack of money (Shortez of money) was now giving trouble to both Dhruv's present and Future, because he has to face suspension many times due to lack of profession in school, Para I mean That he was thrown out of the classes due to non-deposit of money, many times he was sent home, that too with a notice that .... your children this suspended due then not paying fees) .... what was then Slowly, the same memories were making poet memories for him every day and before going to school, he always wished that I should not be thrown out of class today, after a long time, when his condition did not improve, then his destination was , whatever he wanted, they also slowly started powdering with him .... what was then he did a lot of work to go to school sometimes he does not go to school for 2 weeks (weeks), yet everyone in his family forced him (Force) Used to go to school and he never spoke .... but never told anyone the reason why he didn't go nor did anyone Ever tried to ask him what is the reason for not going to school, he knew that everyone was .... but did not want to confess in front of him, childhood is such a hope in which we should never face lies but he was such a boy .... (if I may say, I think his goal was not to move forward, Bash just wanted his family to be well.) Still, forgetting everything, he used to go daily and the same things happened every day and many times he did not even allow him to give the exam because his father had never deposited the full fee .... in childhood, if any reason is found to move back then We consider human reason as our life, when Dhruv was 10 years old, whatever he thought, whatever he wanted to do or say that he wanted to powder everything behind the destination and say no one If a thing is easily found, it becomes a blessing even if it remains ...., but if it is found, do not wish to move forward and keep your mouth .... See the same moment every time Kar Dhruv had thought that the importance of money is also a turn of dreams .... what was after that, he started falling far behind in studies because every time he used to think that the troubles with which he fights every day is ..... How did he get out of it, how to end him .... The eyes that had hoped to move forward Now those eyes had blurred the reason behind Morne .... Was not weakened Bash was looking for hope to stop the condition he was going through And he himself was able to find a reason to stop somewhere, it is a matter of .... $6^{th}$ standard when he first did what he believed to be his death (smoking) one of the reasons was that his problems got worse over time. Know because earlier only profession was the reason but now his body has also become a trouble for him, I mean when he was 12 years old he got a disease called (Marie Antoinette Syndrome Designatius Thee Condition) In which scalp hair suddenly white d After all, a rate had made a place in his value that he would never be able to get out of them .... He says smoking is injurious for health like .... when dreams are went down then it also causes death and injury for our Stability of retarded) .... This cycle continued and finally due to paucity of money and non-payment of fees, you have to leave your school too, that too puree for a year .... A lot happened in that one year to share with Dhruv I don't know how to do left I still want to tell one year because of all the trouble that happened to her, I request that no one else should be .....

"

***"We tried to change the time***
***But Damn shit it changed us ."***"

# IX
# The Peace

*“"Times had changed*
*but not the situation*
*it was the same*
*but now first*

***nothing like***
***What should I say***
***what to hide***
***Conversation is the same***
***but to tell him***
***No longer my tongue."***"

One year... stay when it is deserted or the destination looks even more scary, its meaning is very clear, earlier there were only two reasons for Dhruv, but now another reason has given a different problem in his mind, on which tongue always There used to be a reason for making noise, but now it had become a gathering of silence, the act which used to become the reason for everyone's misery, today it had become the reason for some grocery, the loneliness that the eyes never saw, it became someone's condition. went .... now i will not share his words because my words are not enough to describe his condition in words (so now i am bringing his words in front of you all in the words of what he felt time) I mean he was very fond of writing diary and he used to write every day in his own words in his diary ....

"***"life was not together***
***still hope to live***
***become a gathering of loneliness***
***this heart was lost***
***still someone's shares***
***that we did not do."***"

"***DEAR DIARY,***
***DATE :20/10/2017***
***DAY:FRIDAY***"

A lot has changed in my condition, my words, my tongue, and now this life is not coming to me, I am suffering, I never thought that I would say something like this, but now I can not stop myself because Today my silence is not even with me .... I have become infatuated with anyone but cannot say because my condition does not allow me to tell the things of my heart to him, I am sorry that today I am true to the point where I am first about it. I never used to think, but today I have been thinking, I am very much depressed, I have finished three packets of cigarettes, still I am not getting rest, even if I get sleep, it takes a lot of work time because thinking has become like this now I can't sleep .... If my life goes on like this everyday then I'm sorry I can't live for long how far he has progressed, I am not patient enough to stop myself, the .... silence is becoming more and more like this and this empty room is my life. Have become a part of and because I am considering my illness as an embarrassment and the reason for my condition to grow behind me, I do not know whether there will be any solution for this or not, but now something has to be done, neither this life is letting me live I don't want to die .... I don't want to share my things with anyone but I don't have the courage .... When you tell my condition to someone else, my hope will increase but not my dreams .... Talked to dad, he told me a little more Will have to wait because the condition of the house is not good, don't know when it will stop, still I will try to leave as soon as possible .... Now I have to go because and do not dare to say anything about this thing .... because it hurts me all the time I have ....

# X

# Enlighten The Life

When I listened to his words, it seemed that is it really the reason due to which he remains so upset, lost in himself and neither meeting nor talking to anyone and always waiting for a happy silence, which gives him a lot of trouble.

It is .... that no one can imagine that in the age in which we remain ignorant of all things, we only find happiness all around and which we consider as our childhood, the same age can also become poison (poison) for someone. It was not known .... why these things came to me in Dhruv, I have not really been able to know the reason till today (I have said that there were two reasons for that, one was his studies and the other was his disease, which according to the world today. There is a lot of command but it is said that not everyone is the same in the world) It was not his fault that he became like this at such a young age and may not even blame his family for this because he too was quite unaware of this. May was .... middle class Even a small happiness is a new life for them and even a small trouble is death for them undefi ned may know one thing, that too well let him move on to others and see himself behind them, all those things were giving such a small in him that there is no cure in this world at all .... and many more such things Whose it is necessary to mention, there is a solution to everything in this world but not of misunderstanding .... Dhruv was believing every day that he would no longer be able to move forward like others and with time his words were also taking a different form. Like chirping over small things, getting angry and hiding one's mistake in front of everyone and not talking well to elders, there are many other such things which I should not mention, it is good to move on ..... The reason was accepted by his family and the biggest friend was to his father because he felt that because of him he is not able to go to school, he is not able to get himself treated and the farthest is .... time when more passed So his mentality got worse and he had learned to walk on many wrong things and at that time I felt that there is no hope for him now. The hope of coming back because the hope that he had always seen in his eyes was slowly disappearing now .... neither he spoke well to his parents nor did he talk well to his siblings ....

"

***"There is a feeling of boredom***
***but no reason for silence***
***If you stay, there is a lot to be deceived(2)***
***But the destination is not known."***"

We can fight with everything in this world .... but we can never be afraid of ourselves, he knew very well that he could never be afraid of himself in any condition because he had got used to it and not .... Because of the silence that lives within the four walls, from our own loneliness, from our own defeat, and what made it so .... If we make something the reason for our defeat, then it is not someone else's fault, it is ours It is the only mistake that we are making him our weakness because of fighting because of human reason .... was not so much trouble that another trouble came in his part, his family has given him complete freedom now given complete freedom to do whatever you want Yes you can do it no one will stop you now If it comes, will we end it .... .... I just want to say that if any part of our body gets damaged, then do we cut it off and throw it away. Get him treated .... clothes, bread, food, all this is not necessary for any human being, it is important that he should be with him in those situations in which he is going through, whom he loves very much, but not himself People are called as human beings, but there is no such thing as humanity, .... among the people, now it started happening to Dhruv that if he makes any mistake, his family members do not understand him nor talk with love, he feels so much that his He will be improved by hitting and molesting (I had mentioned this thing earlier also that childhood has no shape and it has no limit, so in this age we should not trouble any child's childhood .... .... then What was the childhood trauma that was creating such anguish for others in me that it was very difficult to solve .... In that one year he did a lot and wrote many things about himself which he felt everyday .... But now is not the right time that I can tell you in its turn ....

"

***"The nights are over***
***but don't know the day***
***There is moisture in these eyes***
***but no reason to stop***
***We are in love***
***but to tell him***
***No respect....***
***silence is mine***
***In memories***
***but to remove it***
***Not ashamed of."*** "

# XI

# The Removal Of Support

If the structure of something deteriorates, then it is very difficult to do it again as before, a year has passed and Dhruv's condition has also been cured, but nothing remains in him as before, neither the thinking nor the same things as before. She didn't laugh nor did she have a sharp mind .... I don't know when he took admission in another school, but he knew for sure that there is nothing in him as before, there was no hope of moving forward, the silence the he puree silence that he endured for years had become his life, wherever he went, his silence would accompany him and the boy who used to top his school every time, now he started spreading, in studies now I did not feel like before nor as before. There was excitement to go to school, to be honest, he didn't want anything from his life, then what happened with the passage of time, there was a further decline in his studies, he started falling behind everyone, teachers made him work in the class room. Used to keep and keep more outside because he did not talk about anyone and his exams used to get so many numbers that because of his family embarrassment, he got bored. used to say that it does not only belong with our family, none of the people used to go to receive his results .... This also became the reason for him to move backward because wherever he progresses, some condition is in front of him. .... .... The boy who never fought with anyone, now he started fighting with everyone, the boy who never bunked classes in his childhood, now he is going to bunk school. felt (they say that if a wound is not treated in time, then it can become the cause of death in the future too .... .... Many times it has happened that he would return only half way and would say that today in school It's a holiday but his brothers don't believe this and keep scolding him or thrashing him to school again .... He didn't know that the day he realizes how wrong he was, the day he won't be able to see eye to eye .... The biggest mistake of our childhood is that we do not have a thing called Patience, we understand the condition but do not want to get out of it, and adult The problem of the Teenagers and old ages is that we do not listen to their words well, only try to end the trouble as soon as possible in some way or the other) ....

**"*SUDDENLY OR UNPATIENCE IS ALWAYS DANGEROUS TO FIND A SOLUTION KEEP PATIENCE AND KEEP WAITING.*"**

After suffering all this continuously, the time had come that the teachers were troubling him because now he had started thinking that he himself was doing something wrong and whatever happened to him in the past was the reason for that. He is himself somewhere, and now he started trying and wanted him to become like before and to a large extent he was also made but I had said .... were happiness but not for the long time .... .... happiness came It was there but not for much time, they say that if you are adopting someone, then you will have to adopt all his good and bad things or memories, he had become like a pole before but who The past was .... .... then the same things started happening (fee problem, not allowing class suspended exams and many more .... .... he lost, felt himself lonely because where he Even he had to face only the embarrassment .... where he used to study coaching, that too every time the same thing would have been a matter of money, class fee. due toh this he was always suspended from class .... After 5 consecutive years he came in $10^{th}$

standard where he gave board exams and after some time his results came and which had a lot of work numbers .... That was the first day when he had tears in his eyes, felt Regret in himself He had misunderstood himself, as if everything was blind in front of his eyes, he did not come out of his room all night, everyone was happy, he finally passed but what was he going through only He himself was the public, this also became another reason which would give him a lot of trouble going forward .... He had made this failure the reason for his death, he started feeling that bash's life is so long, nothing beyond it .... because he Always kept telling himself that life comes only once and we get the chance to move forward only once .... .... Many times he tried to commit suicide but God did not accept it at the time .... .... to his failure He spent a lot of time before death and finally his college life started, due to which he forgets the things of the past. He thought that because the love he was longing for in childhood, now he was going to get it because of some reason, so why stop, we have seen a lot of silence, we also see some happiness, because ahead of it there is a new twist in his life. Came ............

***“"I die all the time***
***kept requesting to come***
***but never came***
***and always thinks to live a little more today***
***What was the reason(2)***
***The god knows my reason for living***
***understand the recommendation of my death"”***

# XII

# Life and Dream

Now Dhruv had a reason to work on his own self to stay away from those silences and also to come out of the pain which he has already suffered in his past, the .... Riya whom he started accepting as his life. He also met .... Riya for the first time in a few days at the wedding of one of his uncle's daughters, but at the time he did not know that she is also in the college where she has taken admission, Riya was also acquitted a few years from Dhruv. And the senior in college was also ...., did not know these things until he saw him for the first time, that too at the wedding of his uncle's daughter (he told me in this millet that he loves a girl and I also did the rest) Like he said that in this age there is no love, only attraction happens and he also understood these things, but for a while he wanted to meet him on .... .... day and in front of him you have feelings and what is that feeling. He also wanted to tell about her, but he did not know that the uncle whose daughter she has come to the wedding is his younger sister. .... What was it then when you feel thirsty, you will not drink water, then what was it, she neither looked ahead nor went straight back and started talking to him .... Now in this I will not tell what happened next, now you only numb next The conversation took place between them ....

Dhruv: "You are from the side of the boys"
Riya: No
Dhruv: "Oh sorry, it was my mistake, I didn't recognize you"
Riya: "It doesn't matter, did you have any work?"
Dhruv .... "he may just be asking where is the exit gate from"
Riya .... "Exit by going straight to the left"
Dhruv .... "thanks"
Riya .... .... you most welcome"

Bash is the only thing I know Kuni Dhruv told me that much what happened in their first meeting .... (Love in the air) Let's find some reason for my hero so that he can move forward in his life May was also happy that he would probably get out of his past .... After that they both met again, good things happened between both of them in their colleges, now Dhruv wanted to forget about his past and wanted to fix everything, that too a human being For whom I thought she was my world, but at the time Riya did not accept it because she was too scared to get into any kind of relationship because there is a secret behind this too which you will come to know later .... even if she is someone Wasn't in a relationship but Dhruv could give his life for Riya and Riya didn't even love him and care which could have died for her (I think friendship always wins in love and friendship) .... And Dhruv's love for Riya grew .... and increased to such an extent that if she does not attend college one day. When I saw him, he used to go to her house to ask why you didn't come today .... Riya knew that Dhruv was in love with her and she also knew how hard she started but she didn't want to confess that she loved him. Doesn't do .... Then when two years have passed, it is not known (and in between Riya passed her $12^{th}$ boards and the very next year Dhruv also got .... with very good marks, don't know really love was the reason ahead of her) To grow or someone else because only god knows these things .... Now it has been a long time for both of them and Dhruv felt that he should tell now what he feels about Riya .... He calls Riya Kiya and said can we meet, I have to tell you something, then Riya also said yes why not but Riya did not know that the thing that she wants to keep Dhruv away from, because she is about his past. I knew everything and she didn't want him to be in trouble again, so she never let him come close to her .... Well let's look ahead Is....

"

***"she is very beautiful***

***But there is a lot of talk"***"

# XIII

# Battle Ends With Saddness

We get more sorrow than we do not get happiness in love, but if Dhruv had known this at the right time, he would never have done this gusto. There is only one love for him and nothing else, it is said that one sided love and one sided deal will always give .... So without taking this scene forward, let me come straight to the point .... I didn't know that to whom he would give his best The world has accepted itself, has given its reason, she never had it, both met on the day Dhruv had called her, then there was a lot of talk between the two, some of those things had memories of her, then some of Riya And in the midst of that, Dhruv had already thought that today I will tell him what is in my heart for sure and yes he did tell, but it was his biggest mistake because he did not know that Riya was in love with him at the time. does not and can never do .... but why the answer will be found only later, but before that let's listen to them .... (by the way It is not necessary to tell anyone's secrets, but it is necessary to share it).

"

***Dhruv: "I have something to say to you..."***
***Riya: "What?"***
***Dhruv: "I have never felt so much for anyone, I mean I can't live without you.."***
***Riya: "But I am with you, idiot"***
***Dhruv: "Yes it is but man it is not the thing that I want to say, there is something else I have to say to you.."***
***Riya ....***
***said something idiot: ...........***
***RIYA: ....***

*Dhruv: "Mmmm.. I love you and I can't live without you even for a moment, because when I saw you for the first time, I thought I should say happy time but I had no courage and no words how to tell you Sorry, you are so late, but my friend can't live without you, because today your words are everywhere, your dreams, that smile of yours, your angry eyes and wake me up in the morning by calling me a fool every day and when I can't do anything, and all this pulls me towards you Last thing is under taken ...love you buddy...love you so much"*

*Riya: (Shocked) Riya: "What are you saying are you mad?"*

*Dhruv .... "Why what happened man, I have only told the things of my heart to you"*

*Riya .... "buddy, I may also say the same thing, May no love for you do .... Look Dhruv you are a very good friend of mine and I love you more than my life but it is not in love, May play with you" I don't want to be with someone else .... This is the worst and worst thing in the world because it works to set fire to even a good relationship, this love is .... See this time you talk about it again What have you become, now there is a whole future ahead of you so please focus on dumb boy..."*

*Dhruv: "So what was that closeness, man, was that not your love?"*

*Rhea .... "no man was nothing"*

*Dhruv: "Oh .. that means I was wrong, I misunderstood everything, that's taking care of you, keeping me away from other girls and always when I try to make someone near to me yet or someone I feel jealous of them. do not speak to me, it was all a lie .... Ohh sorry may now understood was living in what condition I was past what you've been away from me, in may and has not said a second my illness might have caused to you my love Rejecting..."*

*Riya: "What are you saying Dhruv, I want you the most, but not in the way that you want now, you are my life and I can't live without you and your illness is the reason to mind at all." Not there ..."*

*Dhruv: "stop buddy don't show this fake sympathy in front of me, maybe because I have been facing this since childhood .... now I don't have the courage to bear it anymore, thanks for saving under you give to me ( Your Time, Your Complete Love, Your Fake Sympathy And The Last Thing The Broken Heart)..Can't Stop Here Now, Hate Has Been From My Own Troubles, From Your Own Words, And From Your Memories .... Sorry But It's Last The meeting was yours......"*

*Riya .... "Don't do this man, please stop, I can't get used to your silence. Stop because of that, your madness (Riya is speaking .... please don't go, please dont ,go ..)*

*Dhruv: "Stop crying, everyone is watching, and have to take care of yourself. Bye take care...."*

*Riya : .... "Dhruv no .... please buddy beg you don't do .....please dhruv, please dhruv dont go I am sorry buddy .... please.." "*

The wonderful thing is that people do not know about

someone's closeness (closeness) to someone's care, how they give the name of love, and what kind of love is this man, where one's arguments are heard, but the one who is standing on the other side has one. It didn't even matter... After a few days, Dhruv had lost his connection with everything and the things he had forgotten, now he started tormenting him again, and this time those things and his old memories hurt him.

I have given that it is very difficult to tell him in words. There is only silence and nothing .... and he did the same, he left his family without informing .... .... After this, many people started searching for Riya was also with Dhruv's family, everyone was crying in a gray condition It was because Dhruv's call was unrichabale but ist not end .... .... it took many days to do like this, 1 month .... After that everyone felt that Dhruv is no more in this world, he has stolen us .... .... Worst condition Dhruv's mother It was from the father because he did not want to hear that his beta is not with him, but after a month he came but this time a lot had changed such as .... humanity, his personality, his behavior, his being with someone and a lot .... .... when he came everyone got the news everyone came to see him and Riya was also .... but Dhruv did not want to meet them all, so he had locked himself in a room, while waiting, everyone stayed for a long time, then after the evening, he also left, but Riya Didn't go, she tried to understand him a lot, tried to persuade and also said that I am ready to come in a relationship with you, but please man, show your gross, stupid man, .... please man if I am the reason for this what maybe never come but don't hurt yourself like this please .... His condition is not cured for himself) .... After all he did many wrong things like (had affair with many girls, also played with many's heart and what Riya had done with him now she is doing the same thing with someone else While doing this, he started selling liquor bottles to earn money and many times due to this he also went to the police station .... as Dhruv despite all. father kicked Dhruv out of the house and Dhruv took away all those memories, leaving his first love and left everything (after that what happened that Dhruv is no longer with us in this world, and why may I call him his hero) I am, and why Riya who really loved him, why did she consider him at that time, what was the reason, and why is not there in this world, you will know all these things later). Till then wait for the next part ....

*“"Not my dream*
*but his voice is*
*and had prayed himself*
*to replace*
*But at that time my prayer*
*like my dream*
*I was in love with you*
*But in return got the status of loneliness*
*And I was planning to leave in time*
*But soon his planning*
*Made this heart of mine blown....."”*

# The Conclusion

We see many things in a day, we suffer many emotions but never pay attention to that thing because nowadays we give everything behind to move forward (like someone's love, someone's feelings, someone's care) To do, and there are many such things) Childhood would have been the best age that we should stay right and keep it in the future and they say that if the beginning is not good then it becomes a belief that there is nothing better than that .... is not the only family of Dhruv who has gone through all the things and there are many such families who are forced to dream and hope of their own children in China and what is the reason for that only profession. We humanity We do things every day but we never know how to do it. Our country is not poor because we do not have a profession, it is employment because it is not an issue. Can't make things because if they were to be made, they could have made many animals into human beings because life is in them too. Our humanity sees when someone Farmers are getting wasted. By writing two articles, it shows humanity by telecasting those situations.. We all will not even know that in the year 2019, 90000 young adults have been murdered because of mentality and what was the reason why no one knows why us So we have to move forward, we have to work for a profession. If it was happening with Dhruv, if he took the common .... bead all serious then he would never have said this. I just request that if you are grown up in the profession then why don't you help the man who is below you Why don't you keep him with you.. oh yes, I forget to forget the middle class poor, this is also a matter of turning back the humanity of all of us. Knows for unity and that which is not there in us, then why do you speak..

"***time is tight***
***not human...***"

Because we can't change it but we can change ourselves, then why so .... then read the next part of this only when you have fulfilled the duty of being human and saved humanity ....

“

***"No sound of soul without his body***
***in the same way any human identity***
***wouldn’t have happened without humanity....."***”

Printed by Libri Plureos GmbH in Hamburg, Germany